Twinkle, Twinkle, Squiglet Pig

Joyce Dunbar   **Tim Hopgood**

EGMONT

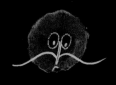

For all creatures weird and wonderful

J.D.

For Julie-Ann, Tim, Josh and Louis

T.H.

First published in Great Britain 2013
by Egmont UK Limited
The Yellow Building,
1 Nicholas Road,
London W11 4AN

www.egmont.co.uk

Text copyright © Joyce Dunbar 2013
Illustrations copyright © Tim Hopgood 2013

The moral rights of the author and illustrator have been asserted

ISBN 978 1 4052 5755 8 (hardback)
ISBN 978 1 4052 5756 5 (paperback)
ISBN 978 1 7803 1339 9 (ebook)

A CIP catalogue record for this title is available from the British Library.

EGMONT LUCKY COIN

Our story began over a century ago, when seventeen-year-old
Egmont Harald Petersen found a coin in the street.

He was on his way to buy a flyswatter, a small hand-operated
printing machine that he then set up in his tiny apartment.

The coin brought him such good luck that today Egmont has
offices in over 30 countries around the world. And that lucky
coin is still kept at the company's head offices in Denmark.

Once, in a place at the bottom of the ocean that is deeper, darker, further, wetter, colder, lonelier than anything you can imagine, there lived a **Piglet Squid.**

Piglet Squid had eight arms, two tentacles,
a snorter for blowing water in and out,
and a big, dreamy, happy

smile!

He smiled all night
in that deep, dark place.
He smiled all day too, though day was
no different from night, because no light
reached those murky depths.

There were other fishes round about,
but they were all so woebegone.

"I can't see what there
is to smile about,"
frowned a hairy frogfish.

"Neither can I,"
whined a wonky-eyed blobfish.

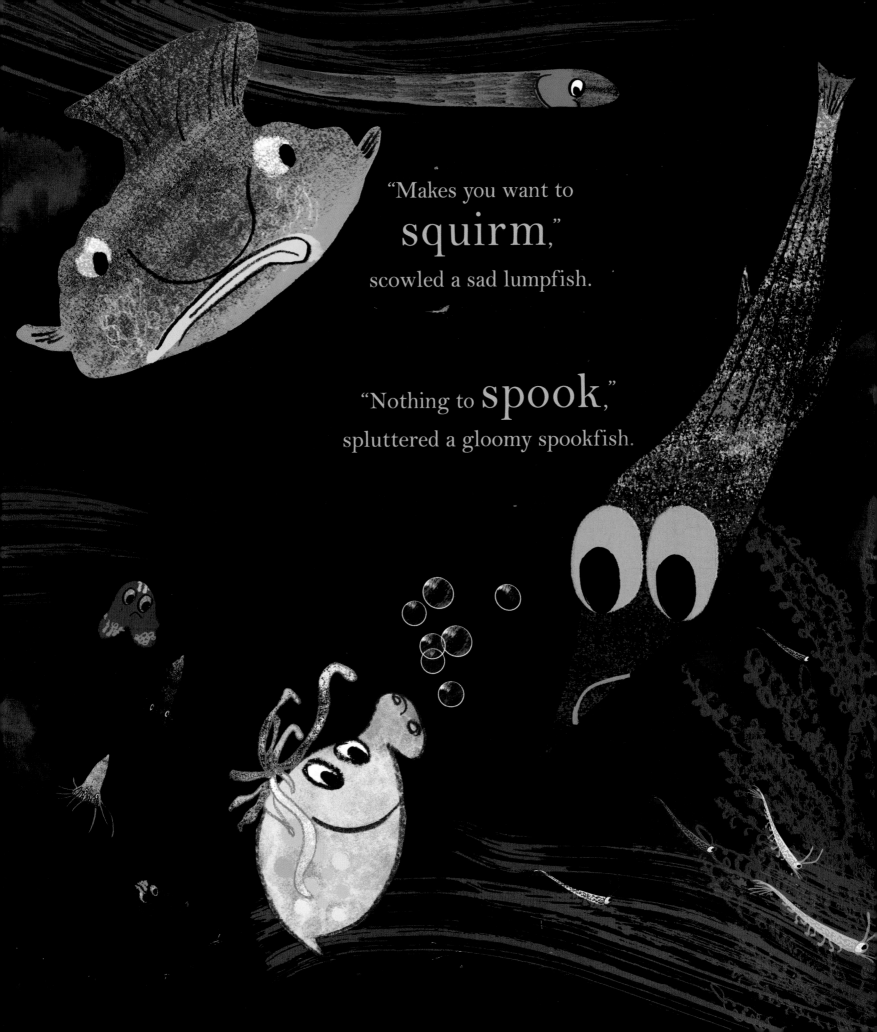

"Makes you want to **squirm**,"
scowled a sad lumpfish.

"Nothing to **spook**,"
spluttered a gloomy spookfish.

"Mutter, mutter,"
moaned a miserable
mola mola.

"Boring, boring,"
sighed a lugubrious
loosejaw.

"Just us!" they blubbed.
"Just this!" they burbled.
"Woe, woe, woe," they mouthed.

And what did
Piglet Squid do?
He smiled.

He smiled at the poor,
sad woebegone fish.
He wished the woebegone
fish would smile back.

One day, Piglet Squid decided to go
in search of something to smile about.
He wanted to tell the woebegone fish all about it.
He floated away from the darkest depths.

Upwards and onwards,
a tiny smile in the great big ocean.

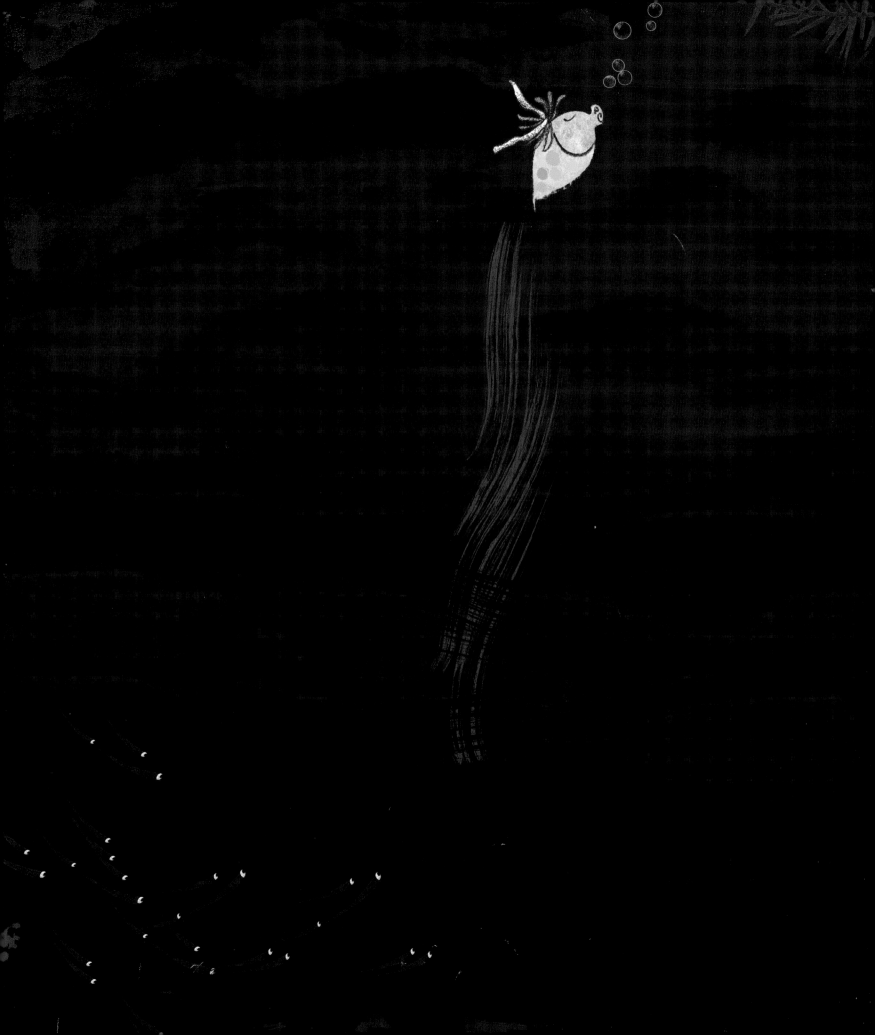

Soon, he met a swallower fish.

"Do you know what there
is to smile about?"
he asked the swallower fish.

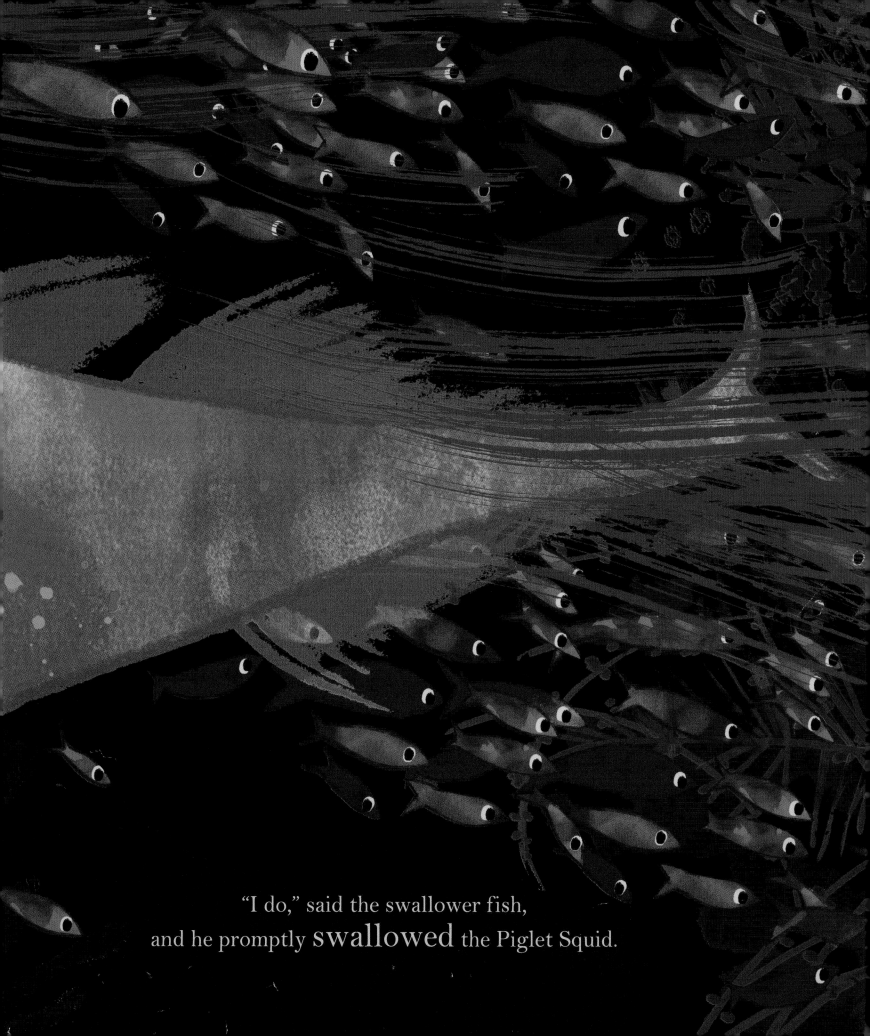

"I do," said the swallower fish,
and he promptly **swallowed** the Piglet Squid.

But the swallower fish wasn't happy for long,
for he was **swallowed** by a coffinfish.

And the coffinfish
was swallowed by . . .

a whale!

So there was Piglet Squid,
inside a swallower fish,
inside a coffinfish,
inside a WHALE!

Still smiling.

A smile inside the belly of a whale.

Piglet Squid did not know where he was,
only that it was **wetter** and **darker**
than ever.

He **squiggled** his
arms into tufts.
He **sucked** in lots of water
with his snorter
and he **blew!**

The swallower fish began to wriggle.

The coffinfish began to jiggle.

The whale's tummy began to tickle.

And the whale giggled.

The whale laughed and then coughed.

He coughed up the coffinfish . . .

who coughed up the swallower fish . . .

who spat out Piglet Squid.

Piglet Squid found himself
bobbing about on the waves.
But only for a moment . . .

For the whale gave one almighty
spurt through his blowhole –
sending a big gushing fountain
up into the night sky,
with the tiny Piglet Squid
floundering in the froth
at the top of it,
still smiling.

And there, in the night sky,
Piglet Squid saw a pearly,
round, shining face,
in a place that is

further,

wider,

quieter,

vaster,

more of a mystery . . .
than anything that can be imagined.

And all around the face,
endlessly shining and twinkling,
were hundreds and thousands,
and millions and billions
of shiny things,
all smiling.

Piglet Squid smiled at the face. The face smiled back. Oh, such a smile!

Somehow, Piglet Squid made his way back
to the deep, dark place in the ocean,
to the place where he lived
amongst the woebegone fish.

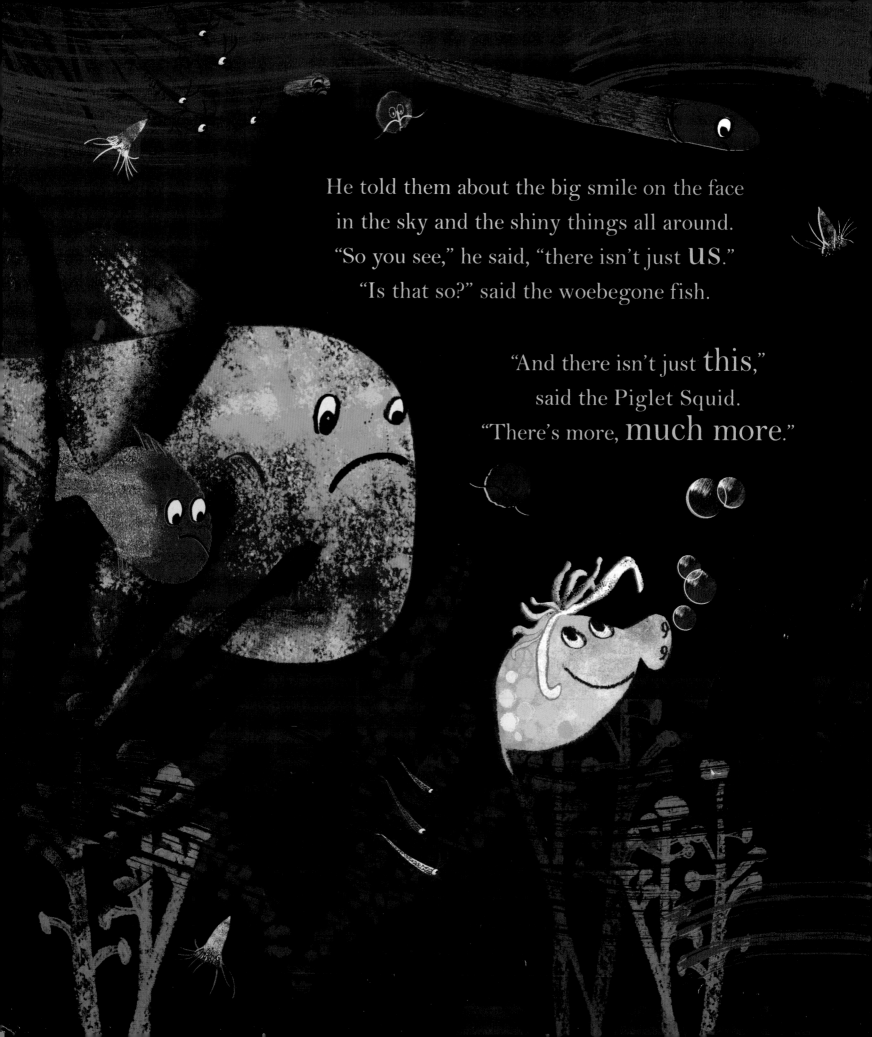

He told them about the big smile on the face
in the sky and the shiny things all around.
"So you see," he said, "there isn't just us."
"Is that so?" said the woebegone fish.

"And there isn't just this,"
said the Piglet Squid.
"There's more, much more."

"And what are these **shiny things** called?" asked the woebegone fish.

Piglet Squid's face crinkled up into a frown. A thinking frown. Then he had a bright idea. "They are called . . .

twinkle, twinkle,
squiglet pigs!"

"That's the **silliest** thing we ever
heard," said the woebegone fish.
Then they did something they had never done before . . .

they smiled!